Dear Ethan,
   I Loved this
book — The drawings are so
comical and the poems are
quite wonderful! I hope
you like it too!
      Love,
      Grandma

for sarah-jane & for pauline
♡ *with my love* ♡

Text and illustrations copyright © 1991 Rodney Rigby
First published in 1991 as *Thare's a building in the city*
by ABC, **A**ll **B**ooks for **C**hildren,
a division of The All Children's Company Ltd
33 Museum Street, London WC1A 1LD
Printed in Hong Kong
First published in the USA by Hyperion Books for Children
114 Fifth Avenue, New York, NY 10011

Library of Congress Cataloging-in-Publication Data
Rigby, Rodney
There's a building on Sixth Avenue / Rodney Rigby. — 1st ed.
p. cm.
Summary: Four-line poems reveal a humorous perspective on their subjects:
Martians, a cowboy, deep-sea diving, the new moon, and many others.
ISBN 1-56282-155-5 (trade), — ISBN 1-56282-156-3 (lib.)
1. Children's poetry. [1. Humorous poetry.] I. Title.
PS3568.I366T48 1991
811'.54 — dc20 91-23097
CIP
AC

There's a Building on Sixth Avenue

RODNEY RIGBY

Hyperion Books for Children
New York

Just Imagine

Imagine you're in outer space,
or a cake that sings a tune,
or lying softly on a cloud
while talking to the moon.

A Castle in Distress

A hurried cry was heard afar
from a castle in distress;
it tried to go 10 miles per hour
but could only go much less.

The Cowboy

A cowboy, tired of wandering,
looked for somewhere soft to sleep;
he caught a couple of passing clouds
and slept without a peep.

The Snowmen

A snowman was sad
with no one to play,
so he made some new friends,
now he plays the whole day.

The Banana Grower

There's a man who wears a sunhat
the color of his suit;
he stands beneath the sun all day
and grows a lot of fruit.

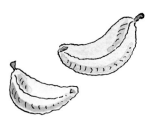

The Shooting Starfish

 Two whales and a passing crab
each were given a wish,
for they had seen a very rare thing—
the shooting starfish.
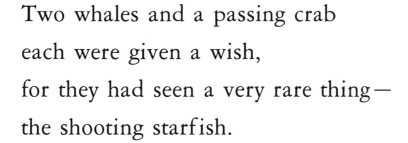

The Explorers

Three intrepid young penguins
went exploring on an ice boat;
two of them took sandwiches
and the other took a warm coat.

The Paper Boat

A paper boat with heart-shaped sails
was gently put to sea;
it sailed the world one thousand times
and returned in time for tea.

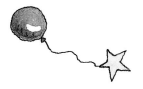

The Balloon Seller

The balloon seller
works by day;
then, come night,
he drifts away.

The Octopus

The octopus is clever
if without a struggle,
it can walk and swim and eat
while learning how to juggle.

There's A Building on Sixth Avenue

There's a building on Sixth Avenue
that comes alive at night —
it looks around for things to do
and gives everyone a fright.

The Wind-up Train

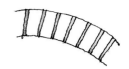

The thing about a wind-up train
that runs along a track
is, that every time it goes away,
it turns and comes right back.

The Biggest Boat

There's a secret to tell
about the biggest boat—
it runs along on wheels
because it's much too big to float.

The Martians

Space-traveling Martians
anxious for sleep,
were heard counting stars
in the absence of sheep.

The Lighthouse Light

Ships young and old,
when out at night,
all look for help
from the lighthouse light.

The Singing Cake

A baker baked a singing cake,
which everyone came to see;
it sang all day for pennies
and, on birthdays, sang for free.

The New Moon

The moon was so tired
from shining all night;
a new moon was found
till the old one shone bright.

The Boat Builder

A man who builds boats
is as happy as can be
when he launches his boats
and they sail out to sea.

Deep-Sea Diving

A mischievous deep-sea diver
liked diving from a height
right into a teacup
to give his mom a fright.

Invisible Man

This invisible man
was as strong as could be;
he pulled in the crowds—
he was something to see!

Night Bus to Cairo

For the night bus to Cairo,
one often has to wait,
for the night bus to Cairo
is often very late.

Early Delivery

While all the world is sleeping,
tucked safely into bed,
there are lots of people working
to bring mail and milk and bread.

TV Detective

In the fight against crime,
there's none so effective
as that star of the show,
the TV detective.

The Full Moon

Smiley moon, happy moon,
full and blue, so bright,
funny moon, laughing moon,
go to sleep, night night.